Steamboat Annie

and the
Thousand-Pound
Catfish

Catherine Wright

illustrated by

Howard Fine

Philomel Books

NEW YORK

Text copyright © 2001 by Catherine Wright

Illustrations copyright © 2001 by Howard Fine

Philomel Books, a division of Penguin Putnam Books for Young Readers,

345 Hudson Street, New York, NY 10014. Philomel Books, Reg. U.S. Pat. & Tm. Off.

Published simultaneously in Canada. Printed in Hong Kong by South China Printing Co. (1988) Ltd.

Book design by Sharon Murray Jacobs. The text is set in sixteen-point point Parade.

The art for this book was created with acrylics on Arches hot press watercolor paper.

Library of Congress Cataloging-in-Publication Data

Wright, Catherine (Catherine E.) Steamboat Annie and the thousand-pound catfish / Catherine Wright;

illustrated by Howard Fine. p. cm. Summary: An ornery giant catfish that does not like singing causes trouble

for the residents of a little town called Pleasant, until Steamboat Annie teaches him a lesson.

[1. Catfishes—Fiction. 2. Tall tales.] I. Fine, Howard, ill. II. Title.

PZ7.W93415 St 2001 [E]—dc21 00-032656

ISBN 0-399-23331-8

1 3 5 7 9 10 8 6 4 2

First Impression

For the child within me, and all the people I love

—C. W.

For my beautiful daughter, Elana

—H. F.

Have you ever heard of Steamboat Annie?
How she was born juggling catfish, grew taller
than the tallest man, Jefferson Jackson,
and beat him in a mayoral race,
a swimming race, an arm wrestle,
and an anchor throw even though
he cheated every single time?

But most of all, have you heard how
Steamboat Annie took on Ernie,
a thousand-pound, mean,
fighting whiskered catfish?

Well, if you don't know, let me tell
you now, it was a fearsome battle,
a fearsome fishing battle.

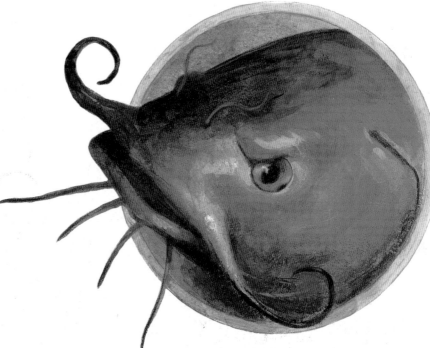

It began in a little town called Pleasant. The folks in

Pleasant were musical, in fact, uncommonly musical.

Babies were born whistling, grandmas played fiddles,

and the children kept time on metal washtubs.

But what the citizens of Pleasant liked best was singing—
the louder the better. Farmers sang and their hens laid eggs,
the teacher sang and the children learned their ABCs, and
when the barber sang not one man wanted a shave.

On Sundays everyone gathered
at church to sing from sunrise to
sunset. Even Pleasant's one lone
cow sang. What a treasure that
cow was as she sang solos in
perfect soprano, her voice
vibrating like an opera singer's,
rippling the waters of the Ohio.

Now it came to be that Ernie—stubborn, ornery, and just plain hot tempered—started eating boats because he didn't like all this singing. Folks sang either too loud or too quiet, too low pitched or too high. Why, the mere sight of Pleasant's singing cow gave Ernie a headache.

So Ernie took to being a nuisance. He ate
Cherry's ferry boat, Little Jimmie's fishing boat,
Tom Sawyer's river raft, Doc's dock, and one night
when a group of carolers were out spreading cheer,
that rascal Ernie swam out of the
Ohio River and ate the church
so Miss Penelope Lacy Brown
couldn't get married.

Folks had had enough. They were discussing tossing Pleasant's singing cow into the river as a peace offering when Steamboat Annie got wind of Ernie's bad behavior.

"This will not do! Pleasant will keep her cow. I'll take care of that rascal Ernie!" Steamboat Annie said.

"I doubt you will," Jefferson Jackson said in his slimy voice. "A woman can't fish, especially for channel cat. Only a man like me who has that wonderful, wormy fishing smell can catch Ernie."

Then off Jefferson slunk, looking for Ernie, thinking sinister, cheating thoughts.

Annie didn't waste a minute. She piloted her boat past the driftwood forest on River Sludge Isle, wiggled through some shallow bends, then stopped at the mouth of Fatman's Creek, where Ernie lived.

"Hey, Ernie, you ornery whiskered catfish, come up from the river bottom! I've got a score to settle," Annie called out.

But Jefferson had beaten her there. Under the water he swam nose to nose with Ernie, making deals and desperate promises.

"That Steamboat Annie has caused me a heap of problems," Jefferson said. "I want to be mayor. I want to win every arm wrestle. If you get rid of Steamboat Annie for me, I'll give you Pleasant's singing cow."

"I've been wantin' a taste of that cow," Ernie said. "Singing gives me earaches; we have a deal. I'll eat Steamboat Annie's riverboat, and if that don't scare her away, then I'll eat her, too!"

Up above the water Annie's voice sounded like a cannon. "Hey, Ernie! I think you're a scaredy cat! Come up from the bottom and face me fair!"

Ernie rose to the top of the water. He looked his meanest, his most ornery, the worst of the worst.

Steamboat Annie took one look at that catfish and said, "There you are, you slimy chicken-belly-ugly fish of a fish. I suggest you leave with a change of attitude before I get mad and fish you out of the river. And take that no-good Jefferson Jackson who is hiding under the water with you!"

"I'll not leave this river, you uppity frog-kissin' steamboat captain! Go home and bake some cookies; you're giving me a headache," Ernie said, and then he spit his lunch of crickets and moss across Annie's best blouse.

"You won't spit on me again, fish breath," Steamboat Annie said. She pulled out her fishing pole, a walnut tree, and tied the largest hook ever made to her line.

"I'll do what I want, elephant ears," Ernie said. He swallowed the anchor, bit off the paddle wheel, and leaped high, mouth open, to eat the smokestacks.

Annie hurled her line through the air. The hook tangled Ernie's whiskers, then fell empty into the water.

"You missed!" Ernie squealed.

"But I never miss twice," Annie replied.

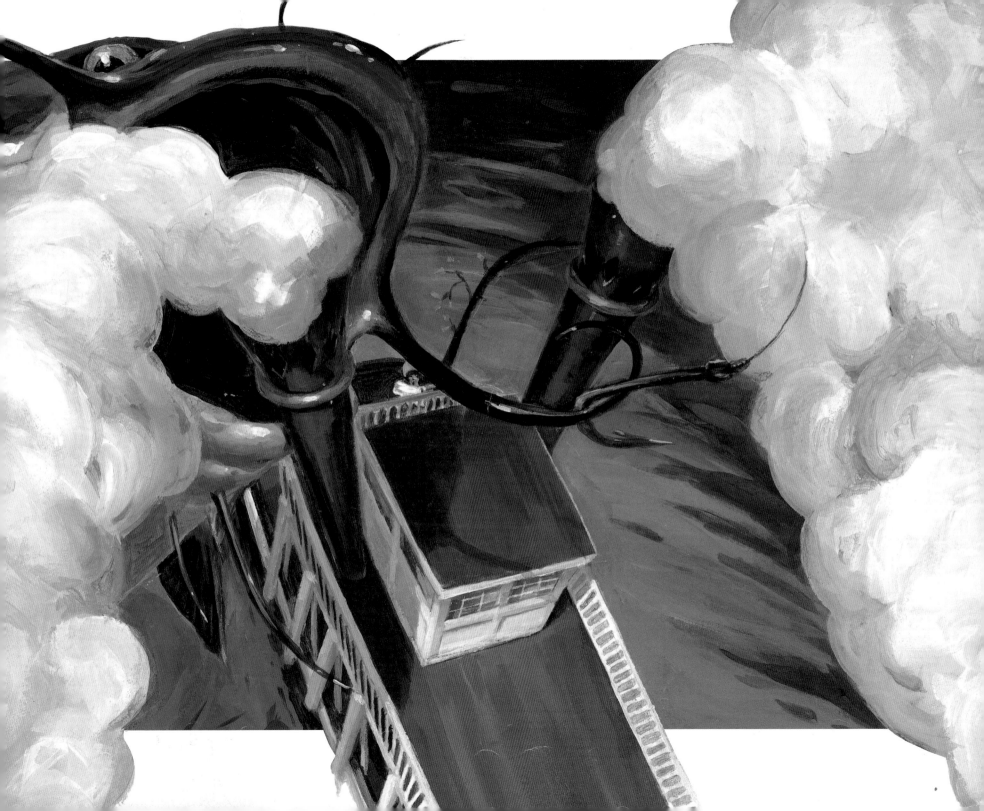

She leaned back hard, whipped her line through the air with a hissing slice, and sunk her hook into that thousand-pound ornery catfish. "Gotcha!" she cried.

"Not for long," Ernie answered as he dove to the river bottom.

He wiggled, splashed, belched mosquitoes, and spit water, but Annie held tight to her fishing pole.

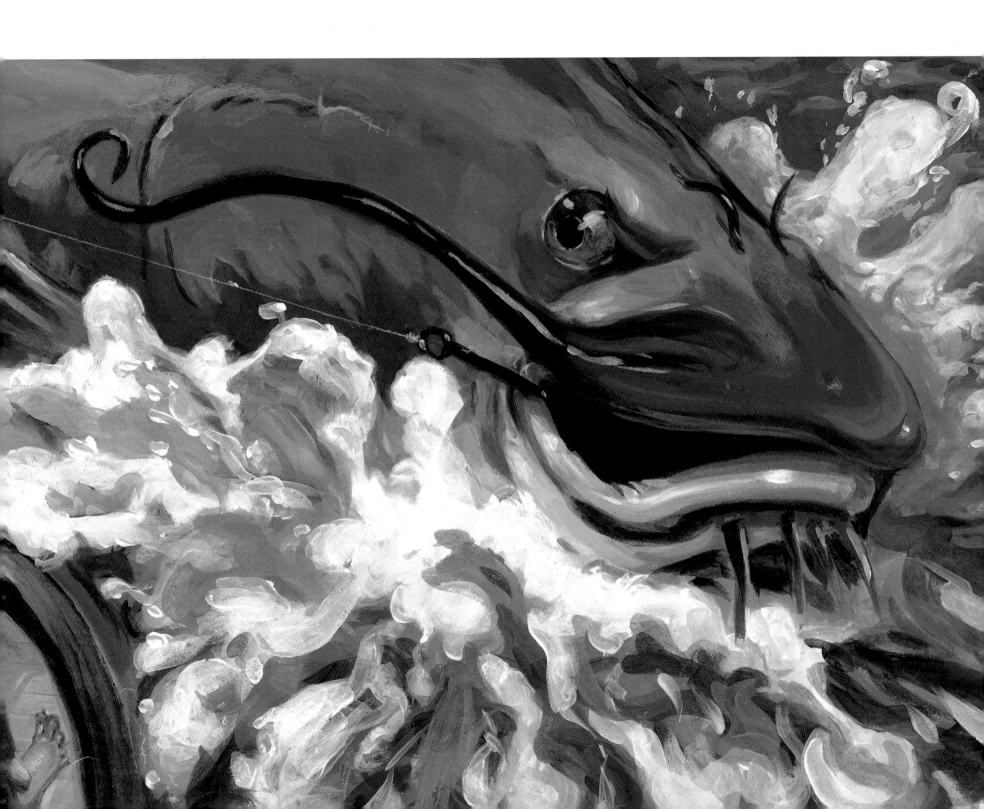

For a year and a half Ernie pulled Annie and her steam-boat down the Ohio, to the mouth of the Mississippi, and back again. People cheered as they passed, had picnics, sold souvenirs, and all the while Annie played the calliope with her toes so that folks would have dancing music.

And then one morning, when the river lay
still like mirror glass, Annie—like every
fisherman who has come before and after
her—felt an instant of slack in her line.

With a quick jerk she pulled Ernie out of the water. Annie twirled that thousand-pound catfish around and around in bigger and bigger circles until it was as high as the clouds.

"I'm getting dizzy, rodeo girl!" Ernie squealed. "I give up!"

"I ought to eat you, but I think you'd make my tummy green," Annie answered as she cut her line. Ernie flew past fields of corn, miles of grassland and buffalo, and then over the Rocky Mountains. He landed in California territory, deep underground in an old gold mine where, some folks say, he's still causing trouble, earthquake trouble.

At home Doc built a new dock, a new ferry for Cherry, a new raft for Tom Sawyer so he'd have a story to tell, a fishing boat for Little Jimmie, a paddle wheel for Annie, and a new church so Miss Penelope Lacy Brown could get married. Pleasant's singing cow sang a solo at the wedding, and Steamboat Annie had a fine party on her steamboat.

Now you might be wondering what happened to Jefferson Jackson. Folks have speculated over the years. Some say he ran away, some say Ernie ate him, and a few insist it was his bones found in Green Devil's Cave. Only Steamboat Annie knew—and she never told—that she pulled him, crying and trembling, from Fatman's Creek and set him to swabbing the deck for the rest of his days. Of course, there were those warm summer nights when Annie, feeling kind and a tad hungry, let Jefferson fish. After all, he did have that wonderful wormy smell.